MOMMY & ME

A CHILDREN'S COLLECTION OF THOUGHTS

by
Laura Mauk

This tender collection
of school-aged children's thoughts
is a testament to the simple love
between a mother and her child.

0 43422 69570 6

Cover Illustration by MarketForce
Typography by MarketForce

Published by Great Quotations Publishing Co.,
Glendale Heights, IL

Library of Congress Catalog Card Number: 97-071651

ISBN 1-56245-311-4

Printed in Hong Kong

INTRODUCTION

Children see the world through different eyes than adults. My own child, a 6th grader at BBC Academy, often reports to me the events of the day. As you will see from the responses of Camille and her schoolmates, their wisdom and wit is tremendous. BBC Academy's children participated in this book and Camille helped me "put it all together", as she called it. She did most of the research, searching the library for quotes, dragging home books and reading things to me as I worked. I thank all the children, teachers and parents who helped in the making of this book.

Laura Mauk

THE MOST IMPORTANT LESSON MY MOTHER HAS TAUGHT ME!

The most important lesson my mother ever taught me was to never drink or smoke when I am older.

Hannah

Age 7 ½

I LOVE MOMMY

THE MOST IMPORTANT LESSON MY MOTHER HAS TAUGHT ME!

My mother taught me to never get in trouble, because it doesn't pay!

David

Age 13

Mommy & Me

THE MOST IMPORTANT LESSON MY MOTHER HAS TAUGHT ME!

My mother taught me to believe and trust in God.

Sean

Age 8 ½

Mommy & Me

THE MOST IMPORTANT LESSON MY MOTHER HAS TAUGHT ME!

The most important lesson my MOMMY taught me was about my daddy.

Mikaela

Age 2 ½

Mommy & Me

THE MOST IMPORTANT LESSON MY MOTHER HAS TAUGHT ME!

My mom has taught me to always be kind to animals and to love everybody and to forgive them if they do wrong.

Nicole

Age 5

Mommy & Me

THE MOST IMPORTANT LESSON MY MOTHER HAS TAUGHT ME!

My mom said I should always be kind to others.

Shunda

Age 6

THE MOST IMPORTANT LESSON MY MOTHER HAS TAUGHT ME!

Mom taught me to never make fun of the way anybody looks, because you can never know if what they are wearing is their best or the only thing they have.

Camille

Age 12

THE MOST IMPORTANT LESSON MY MOTHER HAS TAUGHT ME!

My mom taught me that if you are nice to people they will be nice to you.

Michelle

Age 9

Mommy & Me

THE MOST IMPORTANT LESSON MY MOTHER HAS TAUGHT ME!

I think that the most important lesson my mom taught me was to be honest and always love.

April
Age 12

The most important lesson my mom taught me was to NOT run in the house!

Vicki

Age 6

THE MOST IMPORTANT LESSON MY MOTHER HAS TAUGHT ME!

My mom taught me that she loves me and my brother, even when I am bad.

Eileen

Age 6

Mommy & Me

THE MOST IMPORTANT LESSON MY MOTHER HAS TAUGHT ME!

The most important lesson my mom taught me was to wash the dishes every day!

Melissa

Age 12

THE MOST IMPORTANT LESSON MY MOTHER HAS TAUGHT ME!

The most important lesson my mom taught me was how important it will be for me to grow up and be a wife and mom.

Ginger
Age 11

THE MOST IMPORTANT LESSON MY MOTHER HAS TAUGHT ME!

The most important thing my mother has taught me is to love.

Rachelle

Age 6

Mommy & Me

THE MOST IMPORTANT LESSON MY MOTHER HAS TAUGHT ME!

Eat my dinner all gone so I don't waste food.

Joey
Age 6

Mommy & Me

THE MOST IMPORTANT LESSON MY MOTHER HAS TAUGHT ME!

Don't be mean to anybody!

Jenny
Age 5

Mommy & Me

THE MOST IMPORTANT LESSON MY MOTHER HAS TAUGHT ME!

Mom told me I should always be kind.

Aaron

Age 10

Mommy & Me

THE MOST IMPORTANT LESSON MY MOTHER HAS TAUGHT ME!

The most important lesson my mother taught me was to keep myself clean.

Kiearra

Age 5

Mommy & Me

THE MOST IMPORTANT LESSON MY MOTHER HAS TAUGHT ME!

My mom taught me that the most important lesson was to do homework and to always practice the piano.

Mary

Age 5

Mommy & Me

THE MOST IMPORTANT LESSON MY MOTHER HAS TAUGHT ME!

My mom said that to follow my heart was the most important lesson she could teach me.

Sabrina

Age 15

THE MOST IMPORTANT LESSON MY MOTHER HAS TAUGHT ME!

The most important lesson my mom taught me was how to do chores.

Joey
Age 7

THE MOST IMPORTANT LESSON MY MOTHER HAS TAUGHT ME!

My mom always taught me to be careful and cautious.

Koya
Age 8

Mommy & Me

THE MOST IMPORTANT LESSON MY MOTHER HAS TAUGHT ME!

My mom taught me how to make cookies.

Molly

Age 6

Mommy & Me

WHAT IS THE MOST ENJOYABLE THING
THAT YOU AND YOUR MOM LIKE TO DO?

I like to share things with my mother.

Jim
Age 10

WHAT IS THE MOST ENJOYABLE THING THAT YOU AND YOUR MOM LIKE TO DO?

-work on ceramics.

Sabrina

Age 15

WHAT IS THE MOST ENJOYABLE THING
THAT YOU AND YOUR MOM LIKE TO DO?

I like to go shopping, and go to the movies.

Jamie D
Age 10

Mommy & Me

WHAT IS THE MOST ENJOYABLE THING
THAT YOU AND YOUR MOM LIKE TO DO?

We watch movies together.

Joey
Age 7

Mommy & Me

WHAT IS THE MOST ENJOYABLE THING
THAT YOU AND YOUR MOM LIKE TO DO?

I like to be in Florida together.

Vanessa

Age 9

Mommy & Me

WHAT IS THE MOST ENJOYABLE THING
THAT YOU AND YOUR MOM LIKE TO DO?

We go shopping and then ALWAYS out to eat.

Dave

Age 13

Mommy & Me

WHAT IS THE MOST ENJOYABLE THING
THAT YOU AND YOUR MOM LIKE TO DO?

I like to go horse back riding with my mom, on a trail.

Jessica

Age 9

WHAT IS THE MOST ENJOYABLE THING THAT YOU AND YOUR MOM LIKE TO DO?

We play games together.

Sean

Age 8 ½

Mommy & Me

WHAT IS THE MOST ENJOYABLE THING
THAT YOU AND YOUR MOM LIKE TO DO?

**I like to play soccer
and practice softball with her.**

Jacque
Age 10

Mommy & Me

WHAT IS THE MOST ENJOYABLE THING
THAT YOU AND YOUR MOM LIKE TO DO?

I like to play the fish game with mama.

Mikaela

Age 2 ½

Mommy & Me

WHAT IS THE MOST ENJOYABLE THING
THAT YOU AND YOUR MOM LIKE TO DO?

I like to play games with my mother.

Matt
Age 10

Mommy & Me

WHAT IS THE MOST ENJOYABLE THING THAT YOU AND YOUR MOM LIKE TO DO?

We like to plant flowers together.

Nicole

Age 5

Mommy & Me

WHAT IS THE MOST ENJOYABLE THING
THAT YOU AND YOUR MOM LIKE TO DO?

Me and my mom like to watch movies with my brothers.

Nick

Age 10

Mommy & Me

WHAT IS THE MOST ENJOYABLE THING
THAT YOU AND YOUR MOM LIKE TO DO?

We like to go places together.

Shunda

Age 6

WHAT IS THE MOST ENJOYABLE THING THAT YOU AND YOUR MOM LIKE TO DO?

I like to watch TV with my mom.

Dan

Age 9

Mommy & Me

WHAT IS THE MOST ENJOYABLE THING
THAT YOU AND YOUR MOM LIKE TO DO?

We love to talk together, I think that is the most enjoyable thing we have ever done.

April
Age 12

Mommy & Me

WHAT IS THE MOST ENJOYABLE THING THAT YOU AND YOUR MOM LIKE TO DO?

-spend quality time with her.

Jamie

Age 9

Mommy & Me

WHAT IS THE MOST ENJOYABLE THING THAT YOU AND YOUR MOM LIKE TO DO?

We do crafts and Daisy Scouts together.

Vicki

Age 6

Mommy & Me

WHAT IS THE MOST ENJOYABLE THING THAT YOU AND YOUR MOM LIKE TO DO?

-go to the movies.

Eric

Age 10

WHAT IS THE MOST ENJOYABLE THING THAT YOU AND YOUR MOM LIKE TO DO?

-go shopping for me.

Melissa

Age 12

Mommy & Me

WHAT IS THE MOST ENJOYABLE THING THAT YOU AND YOUR MOM LIKE TO DO?

We like to do puzzles.

Joe

Age 8

Mommy & Me

WHAT IS THE MOST ENJOYABLE THING THAT YOU AND YOUR MOM LIKE TO DO?

-go to the store.

Kelly
Age 10

Mommy & Me

WHAT IS THE MOST ENJOYABLE THING
THAT YOU AND YOUR MOM LIKE TO DO?

We like gardening, cooking, baking, arts, crafts, cleaning and using our imagination!

Ginger

Age 11

WHAT IS THE MOST ENJOYABLE THING
THAT YOU AND YOUR MOM LIKE TO DO?

I like to read and eat chocolate-covered strawberries with her.

Lori

Age 9

Mommy & Me

WHAT IS THE MOST ENJOYABLE THING
THAT YOU AND YOUR MOM LIKE TO DO?

**Occasionally we will have
a ladies day out together.
We walk and talk, shop and share a treat.**

Rachelle

Age 6

WHAT IS THE MOST ENJOYABLE THING THAT YOU AND YOUR MOM LIKE TO DO?

We go to malls or other stores, (everything).

Caitlin

Age 10

Mommy & Me

WHAT IS THE MOST ENJOYABLE THING
THAT YOU AND YOUR MOM LIKE TO DO?

When Dad is out of town, Mom and I go out to dinner and eat any dessert we want!

Camille

Age 12

Mommy & Me

WHAT IS THE MOST ENJOYABLE THING
THAT YOU AND YOUR MOM LIKE TO DO?

I like to do homework, help cook brownies, lemon bars, etc., etc., etc.

Madeline

Age 10

Mommy & Me

WHAT IS THE MOST ENJOYABLE THING THAT YOU AND YOUR MOM LIKE TO DO?

-play tea party!

Jenny

Age 5

Mommy & Me

WHAT IS THE MOST ENJOYABLE THING THAT YOU AND YOUR MOM LIKE TO DO?

I like to play games with my mom.

Will

Age 10

Mommy & Me

WHAT IS THE MOST ENJOYABLE THING
THAT YOU AND YOUR MOM LIKE TO DO?

We like to read together!

Aaron

Age 10

WHAT IS THE MOST ENJOYABLE THING THAT YOU AND YOUR MOM LIKE TO DO?

We like to camp in our backyard when dad is out of town.

Joe

Age 8

WHAT IS THE MOST ENJOYABLE THING
THAT YOU AND YOUR MOM LIKE TO DO?

-going shopping and to the beauty salon.

Kierra

Age 5

Mommy & Me

WHAT IS THE MOST ENJOYABLE THING THAT YOU AND YOUR MOM LIKE TO DO?

-play board games.

Dave

Age 10

Mommy & Me

WHAT IS THE MOST ENJOYABLE THING
THAT YOU AND YOUR MOM LIKE TO DO?

-going shopping, definitely going shopping!

Mary
Age 5

Mommy & Me

WHAT IS THE MOST ENJOYABLE THING THAT YOU AND YOUR MOM LIKE TO DO?

-cook, shop and play games.

Allison

Age 10

Mommy & Me

WHAT IS THE MOST ENJOYABLE THING
THAT YOU AND YOUR MOM LIKE TO DO?

I like to make popcorn with my mom because it tastes good.

Mark

Age 7

WHAT IS THE MOST ENJOYABLE THING
THAT YOU AND YOUR MOM LIKE TO DO?

-pray goodnight prayers with each other.

Joey
Age 6

Mommy & Me

WHAT IS THE MOST ENJOYABLE THING
THAT YOU AND YOUR MOM LIKE TO DO?

-communicating with my mother, school and just anything!

Koya
Age 8

Mommy & Me

WHAT IS THE MOST ENJOYABLE THING
THAT YOU AND YOUR MOM LIKE TO DO?

-to be able to do the household duties like my mom.

Koya
Age 8

Mommy & Me

WHAT IS THE MOST ENJOYABLE THING THAT YOU AND YOUR MOM LIKE TO DO?

I like to take a walk in the summer, just mom and me.

Hannah

Age 7

Mommy & Me

WHAT IS THE MOST ENJOYABLE THING
THAT YOU AND YOUR MOM LIKE TO DO?

**Sometimes we put on a dress
and look nice when daddy comes home.**

Molly
Age 6

Mommy & Me

WHAT IS THE MOST ENJOYABLE THING
THAT YOU AND YOUR MOM LIKE TO DO?

**We like to go to
Gramma and Grampa's house to see them.**

Sarah

Age 3

IN WHAT WAYS WOULD YOU LIKE TO BE LIKE YOUR MOM?

I would like to work at the Sheriff's Department, because that's where my mom works.

Joey
Age 7

IN WHAT WAYS WOULD YOU LIKE TO BE LIKE YOUR MOM?

I would like to be like my mother because she is caring and she is a great mother!

Vanessa

Age 10

Mommy & Me

IN WHAT WAYS WOULD YOU LIKE TO BE LIKE YOUR MOM?

I would like to be kind, just like my mom!

Aaron

Age 10

Mommy & Me

IN WHAT WAYS WOULD YOU LIKE TO BE LIKE YOUR MOM?

I would like to be like my mother because when she was young she had a horse named Skipper, and I wish I had one too.

Jessica P.

Age 10

IN WHAT WAYS WOULD YOU LIKE TO BE LIKE YOUR MOM?

-to be a nurse, like my mom.

Mary
Age 5

IN WHAT WAYS WOULD YOU LIKE TO BE LIKE YOUR MOM?

I would like to be like my mother because she is so pretty.

Jacque
Age 10

IN WHAT WAYS WOULD YOU LIKE TO BE LIKE YOUR MOM?

I hope I will bc as hard working as my mom!

Sabrina

Age 15

IN WHAT WAYS WOULD YOU LIKE TO BE LIKE YOUR MOM?

-my mother is very special to me.

Ashish

Age 9

Mommy & Me

IN WHAT WAYS WOULD YOU LIKE TO BE LIKE YOUR MOM?

I would like to work as hard as she does!

Melissa

Age 12

Mommy & Me

IN WHAT WAYS WOULD YOU LIKE TO BE LIKE YOUR MOM?

I would like to be like my mother because she makes good food!

Matt

Age 10

Mommy & Me

IN WHAT WAYS WOULD YOU LIKE TO BE LIKE YOUR MOM?

When I get older I will cook good food for my kids and my wife.

Joey

Age 6

Mommy & Me

IN WHAT WAYS WOULD YOU LIKE TO BE LIKE YOUR MOM?

I want to be like my mom because she makes a lot of money in her job!

Nick

Age 10

IN WHAT WAYS WOULD YOU LIKE TO BE LIKE YOUR MOM?

I want to be a wise shopper!

Ginger
Age 11

Mommy & Me

IN WHAT WAYS WOULD YOU LIKE TO BE LIKE YOUR MOM?

I would like to be like my mother because she is good at art.

Dan

Age 10

Mommy & Me

IN WHAT WAYS WOULD YOU LIKE TO BE LIKE YOUR MOM?

I would like to be able to cook like my mom.

Hannah

Age 7

Mommy & Me

IN WHAT WAYS WOULD YOU LIKE TO BE LIKE YOUR MOM?

I want to be like my mother because she sets a very good example.

Jamie
Age 10

Mommy & Me

IN WHAT WAYS WOULD YOU LIKE TO BE LIKE YOUR MOM?

I want to work in a pharmacy and count pills!

Vicki

Age 6

IN WHAT WAYS WOULD YOU LIKE TO BE LIKE YOUR MOM?

I want to be like my mother because she has a good job and she has a lot of friends and she travels a lot.

Eric

Age 10

IN WHAT WAYS WOULD YOU LIKE TO BE LIKE YOUR MOM?

She likes to help people and I want to be like that!

Dave

Age 13

Mommy & Me

IN WHAT WAYS WOULD YOU LIKE TO BE LIKE YOUR MOM?

I would like to be like my mom because she knows how to drive a car.

Brian

Age 9

Mommy & Me

IN WHAT WAYS WOULD YOU LIKE TO BE LIKE YOUR MOM?

I would like to be like my mom because I would be more mature!

Dave

Age 10

Mommy & Me

IN WHAT WAYS WOULD YOU LIKE TO BE LIKE YOUR MOM?

**My mom is very loving to others.
I want to be like her.**

Sean

Age 8 ½

Mommy & Me

IN WHAT WAYS WOULD YOU LIKE TO BE LIKE YOUR MOM?

I want to be like my mother because she is very caring.

Kelly

Age 10

Mommy & Me

IN WHAT WAYS WOULD YOU LIKE TO BE LIKE YOUR MOM?

I play with Nicky (pet dog); and shake my head.

Mikaela

Age 2 ½

IN WHAT WAYS WOULD YOU LIKE TO BE LIKE YOUR MOM?

I want to be like my mother because she is always different!

Lori

Age 10

Mommy & Me

IN WHAT WAYS WOULD YOU LIKE TO BE LIKE YOUR MOM?

**I want to grow up and
be a MOMMY just like her.
I want to love and spoil my children
just like she does.**

Nicole

Age 5

Mommy & Me

IN WHAT WAYS WOULD YOU LIKE TO BE LIKE YOUR MOM?

Why would I want to be like my mom?
Because I would spend time with my kids!

Caitlin
Age 10

Mommy & Me

IN WHAT WAYS WOULD YOU LIKE TO BE LIKE YOUR MOM?

I would like to be able to love the way she does.

April
Age 12

IN WHAT WAYS WOULD YOU LIKE TO BE LIKE YOUR MOM?

My mom helps lots of people. She is strict when she has to be, but usually full of love.

Madeline

Age 10

MY MOM IS THE BEST BECAUSE.....

-she gives cookies, kisses and hugs.

Jean

Age 4

Other Titles by Great Quotations

201 Best Things Ever Said
The ABC's of Parenting
African-American Wisdom
As A Cat Thinketh
The Best of Friends
The Birthday Astrologer
Chicken Soup
The Cornerstones of Success
Daddy & Me
Fantastic Father, Dependable Dad
For Mother, A Bouquet of Sentiments
Global Wisdom
Golden Years, Golden Words
Grandma, I Love You
Growing Up in Toyland
Happiness Is Found Along the Way
Hollywords
Hooked on Golf
In Celebration of Women
Inspirations
Interior Design for Idiots
I'm Not Over the Hill
The Lemonade Handbook
Let's Talk Decorating
Life's Lessons
Life's Simple Pleasures
A Lifetime of Love
A Light Heart Lives Long
Midwest Wisdom
Mommy & Me
Mrs. Aesop's Fables
Mother, I Love You
Motivating Quotes for Motivated People
Mrs. Murphy's Laws
Mrs. Webster's Dictionary
My Daughter, My Special Friend
The Other Species
Parenting 101
The Perfect Man
Reflections
Romantic Rhapsody
The Rose Mystique
The Secret Language of Men
The Secret Language of Women
The Secrets in Your Name
Social Disgraces
Some Things Never Change
The Sports Page
Sports Widow
Stress or Sanity
A Teacher Is Better Than Two Books
TeenAge of Insanity
Thanks from the Heart
Things You'll Learn...
Wedding Wonders
Working Woman's World

GREAT QUOTATIONS PUBLISHING COMPANY
Glendale Heights, IL 60139
Phone (630) 582-2800 • Fax (630) 582-2813

Mommy & Me

IN WHAT WAYS WOULD YOU LIKE TO BE LIKE YOUR MOM?

I would like to learn to be an artist and a crafter like my mom.

Rachelle

Age 6

IN WHAT WAYS WOULD YOU LIKE TO BE LIKE YOUR MOM?

My mom is very kind and she gives up her time for us.

Roderick

Age 7

IN WHAT WAYS WOULD YOU LIKE TO BE LIKE YOUR MOM?

I would like to cook, play piano and type like my mom.

Camille

Age 12

Mommy & Me

IN WHAT WAYS WOULD YOU LIKE TO BE LIKE YOUR MOM?

I would like to be like my mother because she never lies.

Matthew

Age 8

Mommy & Me

IN WHAT WAYS WOULD YOU LIKE TO BE LIKE YOUR MOM?

**I think I would like to clean,
and then loving people!**

Jenny
Age 5

Mommy & Me

IN WHAT WAYS WOULD YOU LIKE TO BE LIKE YOUR MOM?

I would like to be like my mother because she is smart!

Kiel

Age 10

Mommy & Me

IN WHAT WAYS WOULD YOU LIKE TO BE LIKE YOUR MOM?

I would like to be a business person, like my mom.

Kiearra

Age 5

IN WHAT WAYS WOULD YOU LIKE TO BE LIKE YOUR MOM?

I would like to be like my mother because she is nice and treats everyone equally.

Will

Age 10

IN WHAT WAYS WOULD YOU LIKE TO BE LIKE YOUR MOM?

I like to dress up just like my MOMMY.

Shunda

Age 6

Mommy & Me

IN WHAT WAYS WOULD YOU LIKE TO BE LIKE YOUR MOM?

**My mother is not selfish or rude.
She supports people's decisions.**

Jim

Age 10

Mommy & Me

IN WHAT WAYS WOULD YOU LIKE TO BE LIKE YOUR MOM?

I would like to by like my mother because she treats me with kindness and respect.

Jamie D.

Age 10

IN WHAT WAYS WOULD YOU LIKE TO BE LIKE YOUR MOM?

I want to teach like my mom.

Jan

Age 8

Mommy & Me

I LOVE MY MOM SO MUCH THAT I WOULD.....

-die in her place.

Sabrina
Age 15

I LOVE MY MOM SO MUCH THAT I WOULD.....

-clean my room even when she doesn't ask me.

Tim

Age 11

I LOVE MY MOM SO MUCH THAT I WOULD.....

-hug her!

Joey

Age 6

Mommy & Me

I LOVE MY MOM SO MUCH THAT I WOULD.....

-care about her and love her forever.

Mary

Age 5

Mommy & Me

I LOVE MY MOM SO MUCH THAT I WOULD.....

-do anything for her.

Dave

Age 13

Mommy & Me

I LOVE MY MOM SO MUCH THAT I WOULD.....

-kiss her and give her hugs!

Vicki

Age 6

Mommy & Me

I LOVE MY MOM SO MUCH THAT I WOULD.....

-clean house for her!
and then walk the dogs.

Camille

Age 12

Mommy & Me

I LOVE MY MOM SO MUCH THAT I WOULD.....

-treat her with respect!

Ginger
Age 11

I LOVE MY MOM SO MUCH THAT I WOULD.....

-hug her and kiss her all day!

Sean

Age 8 ½

I LOVE MY MOM SO MUCH THAT I WOULD.....

-do anything for her.

Melissa
Age 12

Mommy & Me

I LOVE MY MOM SO MUCH THAT I WOULD.....

-I like to sleep in mama's bed.

Mikaela

Age 2 ½

Mommy & Me

I LOVE MY MOM SO MUCH THAT I WOULD.....

-give her a hug, forever.

Hannah

Age 7

Mommy & Me

I LOVE MY MOM SO MUCH THAT I WOULD.....

-help her with her daily work and take care of her if she gets sick.

Nicole

Age 5

I LOVE MY MOM SO MUCH THAT I WOULD.....

-I would die for her!

April
Age 12

Mommy & Me

I LOVE MY MOM SO MUCH THAT I WOULD.....

-KISS HER!

Rachelle

Age 6

Mommy & Me

I LOVE MY MOM SO MUCH THAT I WOULD.....

-do something nice for her.

Jenny

Age 5

Mommy & Me

I LOVE MY MOM SO MUCH THAT I WOULD.....

-I would give her the day off and prepare myself for school!

Kiearra

Age 5

Mommy & Me

I LOVE MY MOM SO MUCH THAT I WOULD.....

-buy her candy and flowers.

Koya
Age 8

Mommy & Me

I LOVE MY MOM SO MUCH THAT I WOULD.....

-like to go to heaven with her.

Shunda

Age 6

Mommy & Me

I LOVE MY MOM SO MUCH THAT I WOULD.....

-love her and always take care of her.

Aaron

Age 10

Mommy & Me

I LOVE MY MOM SO MUCH THAT I WOULD.....

-give her a surprise!

Joey
Age 7

Mommy & Me

I LOVE MY MOM SO MUCH THAT I WOULD.....

**-make her a card myself
instead of buying one at the store.**

Jan

Age 8

Mommy & Me

MY MOM IS THE BEST BECAUSE.....

-because when I need something she is always there for me.

Vanessa

Age 10

Mommy & Me

MY MOM IS THE BEST BECAUSE.....

-she loves me and provides for me.

Koya

Age 8

MY MOM IS THE BEST BECAUSE.....

-I like how my mom lets me have my friends over a lot.

Dan

Age 10

MY MOM IS THE BEST BECAUSE.....

-she is tall and she never burps.

Jean

Age 4

MY MOM IS THE BEST BECAUSE.....

-she is always thoughtful and kind!

Aaron

Age 10

Mommy & Me

MY MOM IS THE BEST BECAUSE.....

-she always plays games with me and she just plays with me.

Jessica

Age 10

MY MOM IS THE BEST BECAUSE.....

-she provides for me, my wants and needs.

Kiearra

Age 5

Mommy & Me

MY MOM IS THE BEST BECAUSE.....

-she is so nice and comforting to me.

Jacque
Age 10

Mommy & Me

MY MOM IS THE BEST BECAUSE.....

-she teaches me to obey and cooks good food!

Joey

Age 6

MY MOM IS THE BEST BECAUSE.....

-she hugs me!

Jenny
Age 5

MY MOM IS THE BEST BECAUSE.....

-the thing I like most about my mother is that she is nice and not stressed.

Matt

Age 10

Mommy & Me

MY MOM IS THE BEST BECAUSE.....

-she takes care of me.

Hannah

Age 7

Mommy & Me

MY MOM IS THE BEST BECAUSE.....

-she always treats my sisters and me equally and she always understands things.

Jamie

Age 10

MY MOM IS THE BEST BECAUSE.....

-she's funny in everything she says and does!

Ginger
Age 11

Mommy & Me

MY MOM IS THE BEST BECAUSE.....

-she's so talented at arts and crafts.

Rachelle

Age 6

MY MOM IS THE BEST BECAUSE.....

-she's my mom and I love her!

Dave

Age 13

I LOVE MOMMY

MY MOM IS THE BEST BECAUSE.....

The thing I like most about my mom is the way she talks to me in her "Yes, we have no bananas!" voice.

Lori

Age 10

Mommy & Me

MY MOM IS THE BEST BECAUSE.....

-she loves me and takes care of me!

Sean

Age 8 ½

Mommy & Me

MY MOM IS THE BEST BECAUSE.....

-she spends time with me.

Caitlin

Age 10

Mommy & Me

MY MOM IS THE BEST BECAUSE.....

-she loves me!

Vicki
Age 6

Mommy & Me

MY MOM IS THE BEST BECAUSE.....

-she is always there for me!

Melissa

Age 12

MY MOM IS THE BEST BECAUSE.....

-she's my best friend.

Mikaela

Age 2 ½

Mommy & Me

MY MOM IS THE BEST BECAUSE.....

-she knows where everything is when the house is messy!

Kiel

Age 10

MY MOM IS THE BEST BECAUSE.....

-she loves me and she is always good to me.

Nicole

Age 5

Mommy & Me

MY MOM IS THE BEST BECAUSE.....

-she takes care of me when I am sick!

Will

Age 10

MY MOM IS THE BEST BECAUSE.....

-she smells nice.

Sheilagh
Age 6

Mommy & Me

MY MOM IS THE BEST BECAUSE.....

-she will come and get me at school if it is raining.

Carolyn
Age 8

MY MOM IS THE BEST BECAUSE.....

-she trusts me to babysit my little sister.

Brent

Age 12

MY MOM IS THE BEST BECAUSE.....

-she has been my mom and dad my whole life!

Sabrina

Age 15

Mommy & Me

MY MOM IS THE BEST BECAUSE.....

-I love her so much.

Shunda

Age 6

Mommy & Me

MY MOM IS THE BEST BECAUSE.....

**-my mom is always there
when I have a tough time in life.**

Jim

Age 10

Mommy & Me

MY MOM IS THE BEST BECAUSE.....

-she loves me, no matter what I do.

April
Age 12

Mommy & Me

MY MOM IS THE BEST BECAUSE.....

-my mom is nice and understanding.

Jamie

Age 10

MY MOM IS THE BEST BECAUSE.....

-when I wear her make-up,
she doesn't get mad at me.

Jan
Age 8